Curious George®
Super Sticker Coloring Book

Designed by Afsoon Razavi

ISBN-13: 978-0-618-99877-7
Printed in Malaysia
TWP 10
4500710881

www.hmhco.com
Visit **www.curiousgeorge.com** for games, activities, party kits, book lists, author info, and more.

THIS WAY
TO THE MONKEYS

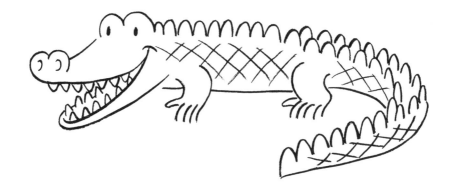

RING TOSS

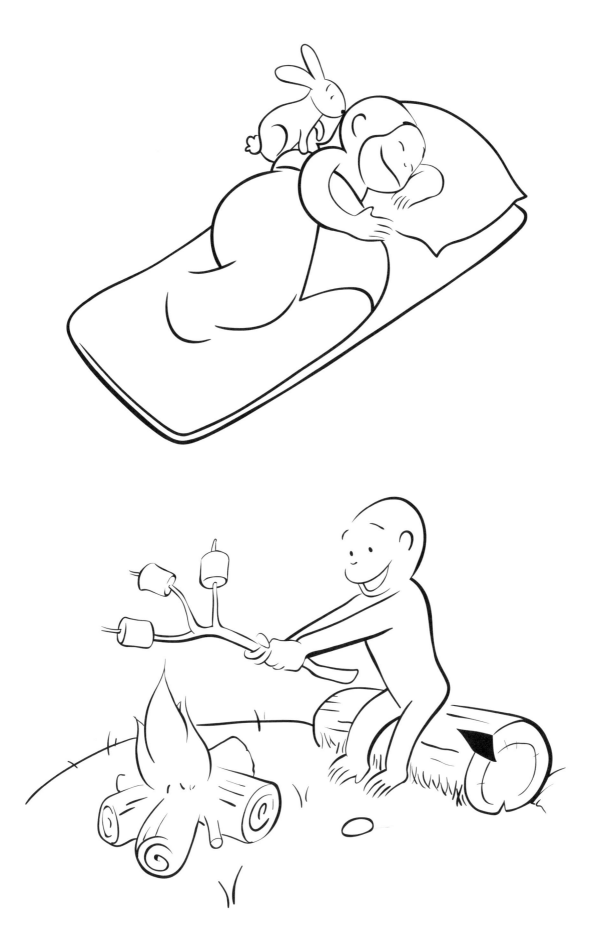

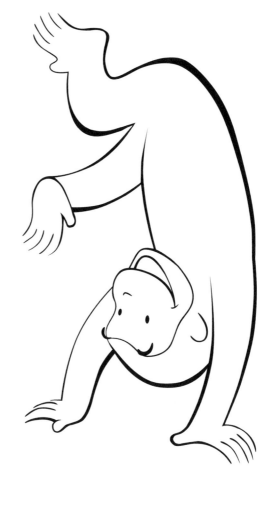

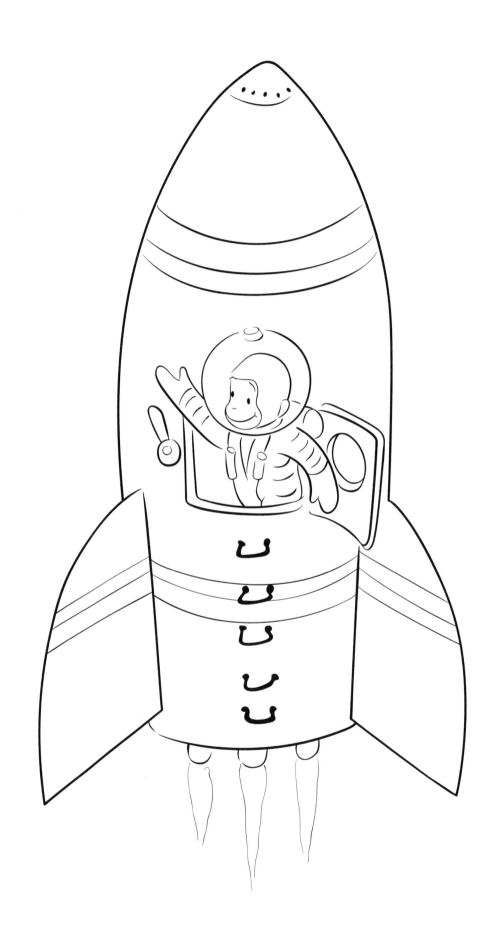

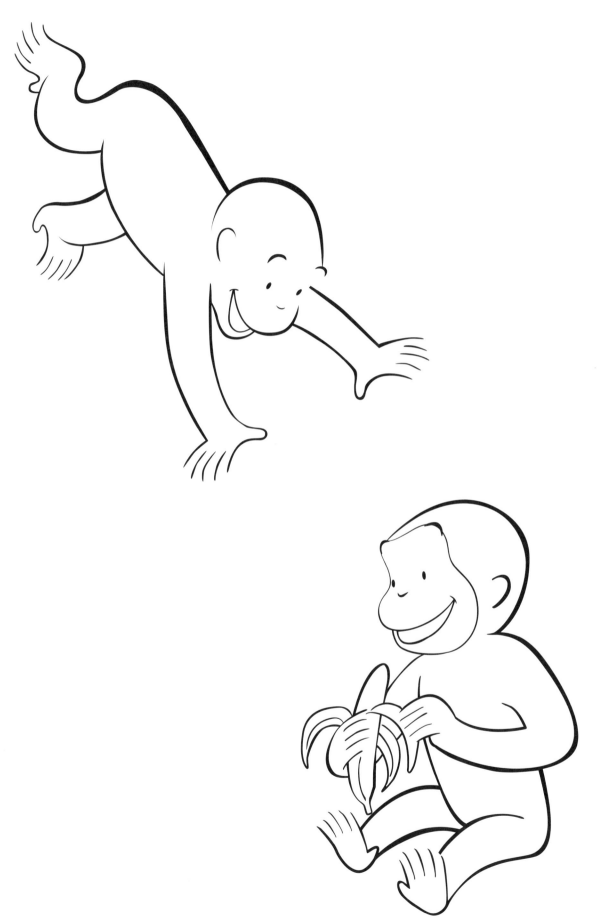